Copyright © 2000 by Nord-Süd Verlag AG, Gossau Zürich, Switzerland
First published in Switzerland under the title E*igentlich wollte er böse sein!*
English translation copyright © 2000 by North-South Books Inc.

All rights reserved. No part of this book may be reproduced or utilized in any form
or by any means, electronic or mechanical, including photocopying,
recording, or any information storage and retrieval system,
without permission in writing from the publisher.

First published in the United States, Great Britain, Canada,
Australia, and New Zealand in 2000 by North-South Books,
an imprint of Nord-Süd Verlag AG, Gossau Zürich, Switzerland.

Distributed in the United States by North-South Books Inc., New York.

Library of Congress Cataloging-in-Publication Data is available.
A CIP catalogue record for this book is available from The British Library.
ISBN 0-7358-1386-8 (trade binding)
1 3 5 7 9 TB 10 8 6 4 2
ISBN 0-7358-1387-6 (library binding)
1 3 5 7 9 LB 10 8 6 4 2
Printed in Belgium

For more information about our books, and the authors and artists
who create them, visit our web site: www.northsouth.com

Danny, the Angry Lion

By Dorothea Lachner
Illustrated by Gusti

Translated by J. Alison James

North-South Books · New York · London

Danny wanted sausages. He wanted sausages and raspberry juice. But today there were only green beans and potatoes. Danny roared with rage and hissed and pushed the plate of beans away. A wild and dangerous gleam shone in Danny's eyes.

Danny sharpened his claws, shook his mane,
and twitched the tip of his tail back and forth.
Danny the Lion was still hungry.

The lion stomped outside and began to hunt.
"But if I don't find sausages and raspberry juice,
I'll eat up anything I can get my paws on!" he
threatened. "I'll start with that man with the bike,
then I'll eat the newspaper lady. I'll have that boy
with the ball for dessert."

The man knelt by his bicycle, sweating. "You came just in time," he said happily. He was not the least bit afraid of the lion. "You see, my bicycle is broken, and I can't fix it by myself. Could you help me?"

Surprised, the lion growled, "Oh, OK. I suppose so." He held the bike steady and handed the man his tools. In just a few minutes, the bike was fixed.

"Thank you very much! You are a very helpful lion," said the man, then he swung himself onto his bike and disappeared around the next corner.

"You're welcome," the lion called.

Now where is that newspaper lady hiding?

The lion looked. There she was, deep under the counter, trying to reach her thermos.

The lion crouched, ready to pounce, as the newspaper lady surfaced.

"Oh my," she cried. "What have we here? A lion with strong legs. You'll run and get me some coffee from the snack bar, won't you?"

"Get you coffee? All right. I'll be as fast as the wind on the savanna," said the lion.

"Not so fast that you spill," said the lady as he raced off. He was back shortly with a freshly filled thermos.

"Thank you," said the newspaper lady. "Would you like a cup of coffee?"

"Coffee? Grrrr!" The lion shook his mane in disgust. He wanted raspberry juice!

But first he would gobble up that boy with the ball.

THUD! The ball flew right into the lion's paws. Well, then, he'd start with the ball.

SNAP! The lion took a big bite.

"Hey, lion! Stop biting my ball," cried the boy.

The leather tasted terrible.
"Give it back, please," said the boy.
The lion dropped the ball.
"Thanks," said the boy. "Do you want to play with me?"

They played football, handball, and pawball. And when they were tired, they went to the boy's house.

His mother was there. "You look like a friendly lion," she said. "I wonder if you would like some sausages and raspberry juice?"

"GRR . . . YOWL! I'd love it," cried the lion. It tasted better than any lion food from Africa to Greenland!

It was as hot as Africa inside Danny's lion skin. He took it off. Hmmm, much more comfortable! Then Danny said thank you and good-bye to his new friends, and went home.

Danny hung the lion skin on the garden fence. But he stuck the claws in his pocket—just in case dinner didn't suit him. Then, whistling happily, he headed up the path to his front door.